BOOKS BY ᴏLIᴊᴀ ᴜ...

Want to know what's next? Connect with Elisa on Facebook, Instagram, and Twitter, and sign up for her free email newsletter at **www.elisabraden.com**, so you don't miss a single new release!

RIGHT PLACE, WRONG DUKE

ELISA BRADEN

CHAPTER ONE

December 19, 1827
Annandale, Scotland

"Are ye certain this is the right place, Lucie?" Lucie Carmichael's cousin Douglas cast her a sidelong glance as he blew into his hands. "I'm nae sayin' ye've a habit of makin' a muddle of things …" He winced. "Well, perhaps I am sayin' that."

Lucie opened the basket Mam had packed for her that morning. *Take this, dearie, and I willnae hear otherwise.* Mam had patted her cheeks with warm, age-spotted hands. *There are wee bits to nibble when ye're feelin' nervy. Mind ye dinnae forget yer gun, now. Cannae carry out an abduction without a gun.* Thinking about her elderly parents choked her up. They'd always taken good care of her. Now, she must take care of them. Nudging aside the pistol, she tore off a piece of bread and popped it in her mouth.

"The maid said he'd be at The Muckle Buck at noon," she answered Douglas, fishing her dead husband's watch from her pocket and gesturing toward the sign above the door. It featured a gigantic stag beside a wee pine. "This is The Muckle Buck. And it's noon."

Douglas shifted, causing the coach to creak like an old man's bones. "Aye. So, where is he?"

She swallowed another bite, but the bread stuck in her throat. Swiping Douglas's flask, she took a stinging swig of whisky and handed it back. "Late, most likely," she rasped. "Dukes dinnae mind makin' anybody wait."

The Muckle Buck—a whitewashed inn typical of those found along the mail roads—sat seven miles northwest of Gretna Green. Most of its patrons were either English couples seeking lodging after a hasty wedding or Scots traveling to England for reasons she couldn't fathom. The Duke of Dingwall was among the latter.

She and Douglas watched the place from inside a borrowed coach. A handful of travelers came and went, none of whom matched the duke's description. *Too* short. *Too ugly. Too female. Too poor.* Her stomach wound into knots as she tore her mother's bread into tiny chunks.

"What time is it now?" Douglas asked, bouncing his knee up and down. "The clouds are gettin' dark. Might snow soon."

She pulled the watch from her pocket and frowned. She shook the thing. Her heart flopped like a gasping fish.

Douglas leaned over to glance at the watch. "Noon? Bluidy hell, Lucie. Did ye forget to wind it?" Swiping a hand over his face, he collapsed back with a groan. "I'm goin' to hang. I kenned I should have gone to Manchester with Rabbie."

She tucked the watch away. It figured that it would be as worthless as the man she'd inherited it from. "The precise hour doesnae matter."

Another groan and a long pull of whisky.

"He must have arrived before we did, so we'll wait for him to exit. Simple enough. The plan hasnae changed."

He capped his flask and shot her a glare. Douglas was younger by several years, wiry, and freckled as the rest of the Galloway family. They'd been raised together, so he was more like a brother than a cousin.

"I wouldnae risk ye," she reassured him. "Nobody will ever ken ye were involved."

Douglas snorted. "Aye, right. This plan will go splendidly. Like yer last one, eh?"

"How was I to predict the solicitor would make off with a dead man's money?"

"Who hired him?"

She paused, wincing at the reminder. "My husband."

"Aye. Yer husband."

They lapsed into silence. A frosty gust rocked the coach. She munched on an oatcake, brushing away crumbs that fell into her decolletage while Douglas drained his flask.

After a long while, she heard, "I'm sorry, Lucie."

She cast him a questioning glance.

"I shouldnae have mentioned …" He grimaced. "It wasnae yer fault ye wed a wormy dung pile."

She focused on the view outside. "Ye're kind to say so, Douglas. But aye. It was."

The inn's door opened just as the first flakes of snow fell. A man—tall, lean, fair-haired, and unreasonably handsome—exited. He donned his hat as the door closed behind him.

Her heart doubled its pounding rhythm. Tossing her oatcake into the basket, she withdrew a folded page from her pocket. She'd torn the Duke of Dingwall's portrait from a periodical. Squinting through the light snowfall, she compared the man's face to the one on the paper. The same lean, hard-cut jaw. The same perfectly refined nose. The same defined lips and elegantly high cheekbones. There was a grace to those features, a beauty rarely seen in a man.

He was a wee bit taller and less paunchy than she'd anticipated—rather fit, actually. She would have thought a portraitist would flatter his handsomeness, not diminish it. He was less fleshy in person. Perhaps he'd reduced.

"Is that him?"

"Aye," she murmured, tucking the portrait away and retrieving her pistol from the basket. "Ready the horses. This willnae take long."

"Are you saying you *don't* intend to take her to bed?" Francis Prescott, the recently minted Earl of Medford, arched an amused brow and drank the rest of his ale. "You disappoint me, old chap. She's desperate for your manly charms. The least you could do is entertain the idea."

"Francis."

"Now, now. I suspect Mrs. Burns could turn your sour into sweet, given the chance. Assuming you don't examine her too closely. Or ask about that large mole on her face."

Silas Northfield tossed back his dram of whisky, poured himself another, and glared at his insouciant half-brother, who thought himself very droll. "She's ten years my senior and twice my weight."

"Well, perhaps she'll find solace with your fatter twin." Francis glanced at Dingwall, who was watching the plump barmaid with the bleary gloss of the highly intoxicated. "She mightn't even notice the difference." The Scottish duke was the only one at their table who couldn't hold his liquor. He was also the only one who grew more tolerable as he got drunker.

Six months after discovering his true parentage, Silas still found his resemblance to these two men strange. True, they'd all been sired by the same man—the previous Earl of Medford. But it was like standing in a hall of mirrors.

"Did he sign the agreement?" Silas asked, gesturing toward Dingwall.

Francis nodded. "Whilst you were visiting the privy and fending off the advances of Mrs. Burns."

"Then what are we still doing here?"

Dingwall blinked and raised his cup. "Drinking?"

"Perhaps we should get His Grace a room," Silas suggested.

"Capital idea. We'll ask Mrs. Burns to tuck him in. She can pretend he's you. I'm certain his wife will thank us for the reprieve." Francis's grin was both amused and brilliant.

Idly, Silas wondered if this was how happiness would look on him, too. They had the same eyes, he and Francis. Would his own eyes dance at a minor jest? Would they settle into warmth as he gazed upon a beloved companion? He didn't know. He'd always been too hungry, too jaded for such contentment. Which was ironic, considering Francis had been raised by a veritable monster, and he'd been raised in a good family by a devoted mother, a kindly father, and a powerful grandfather whose viscountcy would one day belong to him.

Of course, Silas's life hadn't been perfect. His younger brother, Stephen, had been deeply troubled, a problem the family had refused to address. Last spring, Stephen had disappeared and was later presumed dead. It hadn't even been surprising. He'd suffered from unstable moods and blinding headaches for years.

This was the Northfield way: Deny the inconveniences, pretend all is well. Silas's conception was another good example. His mother's affair with Medford had occurred while his father had been away on a hunting excursion in India. Months later, upon Silas's birth, Peter Northfield had claimed Silas as his own, refusing to acknowledge the gossip about his wife or address the obvious resemblance between Medford and Kitty Northfield's firstborn son.

Peter Northfield was a very forgiving man.

Despite having no Northfield blood, Silas remained in direct line for his grandfather's title. That came with expectations. Grandfather wanted his grandsons to share his obsessions with politics and hunting. Silas excelled at both but cared for neither. Likewise, Grandfather encouraged spreading Northfield influence through marriage. He pressed Silas relentlessly to contract an auspicious match, as all Northfields before him had done. Silas half expected Grandfather to send him an instructional guide on propagating heirs for his next birthday.

Even with all the pressures, he had many advantages—vigorous health, handsome looks, wealth, education, a loyal family. His life had been good. He shouldn't be as he was. He shouldn't feel this … starvation.

Francis was Medford's only legitimate son, and he'd suffered untold cruelties at the blackguard's hands. He *should* be the miserable one of their half-brother trio. But while he was sometimes sarcastic and overly amused by his own jests, he was consistently jovial and remarkably good-humored.

Silas had asked him about it once on a ride in Hyde Park. Francis had shrugged lightly and said, "My dear friends Kate and Clarissa would tell you I haven't always been so happy. The right companion makes all the difference. I recommend finding someone who gladdens your heart just by entering a room. Then spend your life ensuring yours is the room they wish to live in." He'd been gazing intently at his valet, George, at the time.

Silas believed there must be more to it than companionship. Something to do with one's underlying character, perhaps. Francis's revelations about Medford's reprehensible nature had been both enlightening and deeply unsettling. Francis had inherited none of their sire's worst qualities.

But Silas had.

He had a calculating nature he'd never quite reconciled with his upbringing. He often blunted it for the sake of others. His unusually strong carnal drives and some of his more wicked predilections appeared to have come through the bloodline, as well. But the quality he feared most was that gnawing void inside him that felt like it could never be satisfied.

He wasn't the only brother with dark inheritances. Francis had confided that Dingwall's casual cruelty reminded him of Medford. Silas took Francis's word for it, as he'd only met their sire twice. Mama had gone out of her way to keep them apart, fearing he'd question the resemblance.

Francis glanced at his watch. "It's half-past two. You'd best be off if you're to reach Carlisle before dark."

Silas's gaze slid to Dingwall. The duke had his chin propped in his hand as he sent a flutter-fingered wave toward a mop propped near the hearth. In fairness, the mop had less wear and tear than Mrs. Burns.

"Not to worry," said Francis. "I'll secure a room for His Grace before I depart for Lockerbie. George asked that I arrive in time for supper." He laughed. "He has a particular itinerary planned for our journey to the Highlands. Imagine the fuss if we're late for Christmas pudding with Kate and Clarissa. George would never forgive me."

Silas paid for their drinks, finished off his whisky, and ignored a hollow twinge. The Northfields seldom gathered for Christmas. Silas usually spent the day alone. "Convey my regards to George and, of course, the MacPhersons."

Francis smiled with that enviable contentment. "Happy Christmas, brother."

Silas exited The Muckle Buck into the frostbitten cold. Snow spun out of nowhere, the flakes tiny and sparse. Donning his hat, he eyed the gray sky and barren fields, the rickety coach parked across the yard.

The less time he spent in this place, the better. Scotland could keep its deuced winters. He gritted his teeth and started across the innyard toward the stable.

No sense in delaying. This was going to be a long, cold ride.

A warm, cushiony body collided with his back. A soft, raspy Scottish voice said, "Oh, I do beg yer pardon, sir. It seems I've had a wee stumble."

He turned. Looked. And hardened to pure stone.

She was tall—taller than his shoulder and abundantly curved in all the best ways. Her mantle hung open. Her red velvet dress was too tight, forcing her bosom to pillow up almost obscenely.

Good God, those breasts would fill his hands twice over and still leave second helpings for his mouth. Freckles made them appear to be sprinkled with cinnamon. He *loved* cinnamon.

Hunger deepened to a grinding howl.

He couldn't see much of her face, which was veiled with black netting. Her mantle and bonnet were black, as well. Half-mourning, perhaps? That would make the red dress a peculiar choice.

"Think nothing of it," he murmured, facing her fully and tipping his hat. "May I be of service in some way? Perhaps I could help you … mount." He wondered what would happen if her bodice failed to hold its position. If it slipped—entirely by accident, mind. Would her nipples slide free? Would she protest, or would she invite him to have a taste?

"Oh, aye. Ye'll be of service."

He was focused on her breathtaking breasts, so he didn't immediately see the gun. Then he slid his gaze down and discovered what she held in her dainty, gloved hand.

"But, first, I'll need ye to join me, Yer Grace."

He frowned, tilting his head as he eyed the weapon. It was a single-barreled, snub-nosed pistol of the sort ladies and fops had favored twenty years ago. It hadn't been cleaned in some time.

"Two problems, love." He bit back a smile. "I'm not a duke. So, your honorific, while flattering, is unnecessary."

Those bountiful breasts started heaving at a rapid pace.

"Secondly, your gun is—"

"I ken who ye are, Dingwall. And I ken what ye have planned."

"I'm afraid you're mistaken. I am not the Duke of—"

"Haud yer wheesht!" she hissed. Her gun hand trembled. He fancied he could see the skin on her breasts pulsing with every beat of her racing heart.

Generously, he offered her a chance to retreat. "You don't want to do this. It's warm inside. Why don't we have a drink together, hmm? The ale is abominable, but the whisky isn't too bad."

"Quiet. I say where we go. I'm the one with the gun."

"Yes, about that—"

"Ye'll be comin' with me, Yer Grace."

Again, he glanced at the falling snow then at the red-dressed woman who grew more nervous—and more intriguing—by the second. This could be interesting. Certainly more interesting than a two-hour ride to Carlisle. Or anything else he might have planned for the night.

"Very well, love. I'm your prisoner. Take me anywhere you like."

CHAPTER TWO

L ucie followed the duke to the coach. "Get in," she said, hating the breathless quiver in her voice. She swallowed and firmed her belly. "Now."

The devil smiled and did as she asked. Well, demanded, really. She'd never been comfortable ordering people about, even when they deserved it. After a quick look around to ensure nobody saw them leave, she signaled to the scarf-wrapped Douglas and climbed inside.

As soon as they rocked into motion, the duke said, "You do realize abducting a duke is a hanging offense."

She adjusted her grip on the gun and swallowed against a dry throat. "I'm not daft."

"No, of course not. I only mention it because you seem quite young. It would be a shame to end your life before you've seen the other side of twenty."

"I'm six-and-twenty. And I ken ye think ye're very clever for drawin' that out of me, Yer Grace, but I dinnae care if ye learn my age. Ye'll ken who I am soon enough."

"Will I, now? That's intriguing." He propped his elbow on his arm and rubbed his lower lip with his thumb. "Will I see you without the veil, too?"

"I find it a wee bit aggravatin'. So, aye. Ye might."

"Seems only fair. You have me at a disadvantage." He stroked that lip again. Stroke, stroke, stroke. Back and forth. Light and slow. "Is the veil merely a disguise, or are you a widow?"

She debated how much to reveal. Her speech contained an entire section dedicated to her family's history, so it likely didn't matter whether she told him the truth now or later. "I'm a widow."

His smile started slowly. She missed it at first, thinking it was a trick of the shifting light. But it wasn't. His hand fell away, and those vivid blue eyes started glowing like a scorching summer day. Indeed, she felt flushed. Burned.

"Oh, love." His smile widened, causing his eyes to crinkle at the corners. "You probably shouldn't have told me that."

A wee thrill of fear—or something like fear—rippled through her. "I told ye, it doesnae matter how much ye learn about me."

"Then tell me everything."

"Not yet." She threw open the hinged basket and reached for an oatcake. She offered him half, but he shook his head, looking amused. "We'll reach our destination soon," she said. "I'll say everythin' I mean to say then."

He crossed his arms over his chest, pulling his sleeves taut over shockingly defined muscles. His Grace really had turned over a new leaf. Of course, he was eyeing her oatcake with a queer, ravenous look in his eye. Perhaps the deprivations necessary to reduce caused him to experience cravings.

"Are ye certain ye dinnae want anythin' to eat, Yer Grace?"

His eyes flew up from her oatcake to her face. Or, rather, her veil. "No." He grinned. "Though, it's good of you to offer."

"I'm abductin' ye, not torturin' ye."

"Define torture."

He must be referring to his efforts to reduce. "Look, ye've done well to improve yerself. Reducin' isnae easy. But one wee bite will do ye no harm. There's ample food to choose from. Mam's baskets are always full to brimmin'."

His lips tightened for the briefest second. "Your mother packed you a basket?"

"Oh, aye." She smiled. "She makes sure I dinnae go hungry."

His gaze narrowed. "Does she know what you're doing?"

"No." Lucie straightened. "Nobody is doin' this but me."

"You and whoever is driving the coach."

"That's a hired lad. He doesnae ken anythin'."

He went back to staring at her oatcakes, seemingly fascinated by every morsel. Long minutes passed in which the only sounds were the horses, the creaking of the coach, and the rustle of the duke shifting in his seat. Given the hunger in his gaze, she expected to hear his stomach growl. Finally, he licked his beautifully defined lips and said, "You dropped some crumbs"—he gestured toward his chest—"just here."

She glanced down. Several oats were scattered in her decolletage. She brushed at the mess with her gun hand before realizing how he'd distracted her. Immediately, she trained the pistol on him, but he didn't seem to be paying attention. Instead, he was focused outside, where snow was turning the fields white. He braced his elbow on the window. His fist clenched over and over. He looked … powerful. And frustrated.

She swallowed hard, wondering if this fit, hungry duke wasn't far more dangerous than she'd originally calculated. Another wee thrill winnowed down her spine, causing gooseflesh to rise on her skin. Her nipples peaked against the tight confines of her bodice. As she examined the duke's clenching fist, a strange tension stirred inside her belly. The muscles in his forearm flexed. His fingers tightened, loosened, and the process repeated. *Tighten and relax. Tighten and relax. Tighten and relax.*

Why was her heart pounding so loudly? She could scarcely hear her own thoughts.

Relief flooded in as she spied the stout, stone square of Hartfell Lodge. "Almost there, Yer Grace," she murmured.

That fist clenched harder.

Within minutes, Douglas pulled the coach to a halt near the lodge's main entrance. Lucie disembarked then motioned with her gun for the duke to follow suit. He unfolded from his position with suspicious slowness, like an old man standing after a long nap in a reading chair.

She ushered him inside, carrying her mother's basket with her. The place was still furnished, despite being for sale. Douglas had worked here as a footman for several years before the previous owner died. He'd kept one of the keys upon his dismissal.

Now, Douglas handed down her valise and the key, glancing worriedly at the door. "Horses are in the stable. Take 'em with ye when ye go. Good luck, Lucie," he whispered before clicking his tongue and driving away.

She carried her valise inside. The duke was there, leaning one muscular shoulder against a fluted column near the entrance hall's main passage.

"Is he gone?" he asked.

"Aye. Nobody else will come save ye. This place has sat empty for months."

He nodded. "Perhaps now, you'll remove the veil, hmm?"

She swallowed, feeling parched. "Shall I make tea? I'm a wee bit—"

"Come, come. Don't lose your courage. You did promise to reveal all once we'd reached our destination."

He wasn't wrong. Plucking the pins from her bonnet, she piled them on a table beneath one of the windows and lifted her hat and veil off all at once. The light brightened from gray to white. Suddenly, she could see him clearly.

And what she saw made her body seize up in one long, bewildering shiver.

She'd thought his eyes were hungry before. Now, they glowed with such a consuming fire, she felt as pinned as a bonnet, fastened in place and put on display.

"Tell me your name," he commanded in a deep, roughened rasp.

She opened her mouth before she could think. "Lucie."

"Lucie," he repeated, rolling the word inside his mouth as though savoring a sweet treat. "Lucie what?"

"Carmichael."

A slow, wicked grin curved his perfect mouth. His tongue flickered over just the corner. "Lucie Carmichael." He inclined his head. "It is my sincere pleasure to make your acquaintance, love."

Her heart was pounding. Pounding. *Pounding.* So hard, she felt dizzy. "We—we must … I have a great deal to say to ye, Yer Grace."

"I'm certain you do." He started toward her in long, devouring strides.

She scrambled backward, her heart panicky and fast. Then she remembered she held a gun. She'd forgotten while he'd been staring at her with that ravenous gaze. The pistol was in her hand, which hung at her side. She tried to raise it, but he was right there. Right. There.

He clasped her wrist in his fingers. Clasped the gun and tore it free. Turned it this way and that before handing it back to her. "Love, next time you hold a man hostage, I suggest loading your weapon."

Her jaw went slack. She stared at the pistol. The one he'd returned. The one he'd known was harmless for the entirety of their exchange.

"Because when you don't," he murmured in her ear, "that man will easily gain the upper hand." This time, his grip on her wrists was firm. He spun her around, pinning both of her arms behind her back and holding her in place with one hand wrapped around her wrists. He plucked away the pistol, slapped it down beside her bonnet, and yanked her back into his hard, infuriated body.

She gasped. Struggled to free her arms. Arched against his hold.

His hold was absolute. His other arm banded across her waist as his jaw nuzzled hers from behind. "Now, then. Let's find a bed, shall we?"

She fought him admirably while he carried her upstairs. She fought harder when he threw her on the bed, and harder still when he used drapery ties to bind her wrists to the bedposts. But every scratch, kick, and curse had been worth it.

She was bloody magnificent.

"I'll blind ye, ye miserable whoreson! I'll claw those blue eyes from yer heid if ye so much as—"

"Calm down, Lucie," he ordered, rifling through the odd assortment he'd found in her pockets. "I'm not going to harm you."

First was a portrait of Dingwall torn from one of those fashion periodicals masquerading as important critiques of art, theatre, and London life. He tossed it aside.

"That is, unless you continue screeching at the top of your lungs. Then I might bind your mouth as well as your hands."

The next item was a folded wad of papers. They appeared to be notes for a speech. He tossed them aside, as well.

"And I reserve the right to seduce you. With your eager participation, of course. I'm not a barbarian."

The third item was a watch. He opened the cover and found an inscription inside: *To my new husband. May these first hours of marriage foretell the joys to come. Your loving bri-*

He frowned. "What happened to the rest of the inscription?"

Fuming silence.

He held up the watch. "Lucie?"

"I ran out of room."

"You didn't consider a shorter version? Or perhaps plan it out in advance?"

With a mulish expression, she turned her head to stare through the window.

The chamber was mostly white—white paneled walls, a white marble mantel, white sheer curtains. But the massive bed was dark-stained oak with four spiral-carved posts and gold draperies. The sofa near the fireplace and the chairs flanking the window were upholstered in the same gold silk.

He retrieved one of the chairs and dragged it to her bedside. He'd taken time to build a fire after binding her, which was warming the room nicely. After removing his overcoat and tailcoat, he rolled up his shirtsleeves and sat, bracing his elbows on his knees.

Lucie's tight red gown looked stunning amidst all that shimmery gold damask. Black beadwork stitched along the edges of the bodice glittered whenever she breathed. But the frock paled in comparison to the woman. She wasn't beautiful. She was luscious. Her hair was the same color as the bedposts—dark, spiraling brown. Her soft, tiny nose was freckled from bridge to tip. Her brows were straight and dark over hooded, dove-gray eyes. Her mouth was a gentle curve with a sweet, vulnerable mobility he'd never seen before. He wanted to kiss her so badly, his mouth watered.

"Now, then," he began, permitting himself the brief indulgence of watching her breasts struggle for freedom from her bodice. He silently cheered on the revolution. "Allow me to introduce myself properly. I am Silas Northfield."

She opened her mouth to protest, but he settled a finger over those delectable lips.

"You assumed I was Dingwall because we look similar. I understand. But I am not him, and he is not me." He retrieved the portrait from near her foot, unfolding and displaying it beside his own face. "See the differences?"

Her brow crinkled into a scowl. "I see a liar who'd say anythin' to escape—"

"I've no need to escape. I have you precisely where I want you."

"Ye're a worthless—"

He held up the portrait again. "He's older by five years. He's shorter by three inches. He's heavier by two stone. He's stupider by every measure. And he can't hold his liquor. We. Are not. The same."

"Then why do ye *look* the same?"

"Because we were fathered by the same man."

She lapsed into silence. Stubborn, Scottish silence.

He sighed. "Why don't you tell me what you wanted from him? What prompted the abduction? Apart from shortsightedness, I mean."

Glaring gray eyes focused on him. "Ye're plannin' to evict my kin from our home."

He frowned. "Not I. Dingwall. And what do you mean by evict?"

"The usual definition. Our house—the house where my father was born and his father before him—sits on yer land."

"The duke's land."

"Fine. The Duke of Dingwall's land. We're to be out by Christmas." That vulnerable lower lip began to quiver. "Christmas! Ye unfeelin' whoreson."

Blowing out a breath, he sat back and raked both hands through his hair. "Dingwall has a bit of a cruel streak."

"He has a yearnin' for sheep!"

Silas blinked.

"He wants to turn our lands into sheep farms and run the old tenants off to places like Manchester," she clarified. "He wants to make his land more profitable at the expense of good, honest Scots who never caused him a bit of bother."

"Ah, Lucie." He shook his head. "What did you think would happen? Did you imagine he'd reverse himself? A man like Dingwall doesn't change his mind."

"I had a speech prepared. It's quite stirrin'. The end has a wee touch of poetry." She sniffed, her lip firming. "Also, I ken he isnae his father's son. I planned to hold that over his head, if need be."

He noticed she'd begun separating Dingwall from Silas in her mind. Good. One less barrier to having her beneath him moaning his name. His *real* name. "Blackmail is a dangerous game, love." He brushed a spiral of hair from her forehead, lingering along her brow. "Where did you acquire the information?"

"A maid. She had a dalliance with him, and he treated her poorly. She told me out of spite." She examined him closely, gray eyes calm and serious. After a long silence, she murmured, "Ye really aren't him, are ye?"

"No. I'm really not."

Her brow crumpled. Her eyes filled. Her soft little nose turned red.

And Silas panicked.

He never panicked. Not even when his mother had told him about the affair.

"Oh, God. Lucie, do *not* cry. Don't."

Her lips quivered. The tears overflowed. She closed her eyes and turned her head as little streams flowed down her cheeks.

"Bloody hell. Stop. Bloody hell!" He climbed onto the bed and untied her wrists. Instantly, she curled into a ball, her body heaving with piteous gasps. Every one felt like a knife in his gut.

He didn't know how to stop it. In his panic, he did the only thing he could think of: He lay down beside her, wrapped his arms around her, and squeezed.

More gasping. She rolled over to face him and buried her wet face in his shoulder. She dug her fingers into his chest and gripped handfuls of his waistcoat. "I … thought … that I … was helping." Her pauses were shuddering breaths. "But I'm nothin' but a … great … disaster."

"Right. You probably shouldn't have abducted anyone, particularly a duke."

She sobbed harder.

He grimaced. "And, in hindsight, trapping yourself alone in an empty house in the middle of nowhere with a stranger while failing to load your only means of protection is *probably* a sound plan for being ravished. And you should *probably* never do anything like this again. Ever."

She wiped her eyes and nose on his very expensive French silk waistcoat and drew a shuddering breath. "Is there a 'but' comin' soon?"

"No."

"Ye're not very good at comfortin', are ye?"

"I don't find lies comforting. Do you?"

A sigh. "No. Well, maybe a wee bit."

He considered several possible ways to soften his points with a "but"—something true yet comforting. Clearing his throat, he offered, "Your overall plan was foolhardy. *But* the red dress was a masterstroke."

She stilled. Sniffed. "How so?"

"I was riveted. And the tightness across the bosom? A perfect lure. Genius."

"I wore this gown because it's the finest one I own. I also wore it to my husband's funeral, though his solicitor thought me vulgar."

"Well, it's riveting."

"And the bodice is a wee bit tight, but I cannae claim any purposeful aim. I measured wrong when I was sewin' it." Sniff. She snuggled deeper into him, making his cock stand up and take notice. Bloody hell, she made him ache.

"However it occurred," he said tightly, "it worked. I was driven to distraction."

"That's rubbish." She pushed away and rolled to the opposite side of the bed to sit on the edge with her back turned.

The chill where her warmth had just been sent his mood into the black. He rolled onto his feet, scowling at the woman who'd invoked his hunger faster than any female he'd ever known. "How is it rubbish?"

She shook her head and removed the two remaining pins keeping her hair from tumbling down around her shoulders. When they were gone, the spiraling mass sprang free in a wild profusion. She fluffed the enchanting curls with her fingers and stood to face him, all freckled red nose, puffy gray eyes, and bristling pride.

Raising her chin, she swiped a knuckle beneath her eye. "I'm not some virginal lass ye can hoodwink with a few bonnie words. I had a husband. He was worthless and deceitful, aye. But he was a man. Well, male. I ken what men prefer, and I ken that isnae me."

For the second time that day, she stunned him into wordlessness. She couldn't possibly believe such rot.

"I'm thirsty, Mr. Northfield," she said, shaking out her skirts. "I'm headed to the kitchen to make tea. Would ye care to join me?"

CHAPTER THREE

The way Silas Northfield watched her gave Lucie shivers from her scalp to the soles of her feet. The feeling wasn't unpleasant. It felt a bit like being outdoors during a lightning storm—dangerous and electrifying.

She couldn't decide what to make of it.

At the moment, he was watching her pour tea into two white cups. She'd spent the past twenty minutes pottering around the large kitchen, making tea, arranging some of Mam's ginger biscuits on a wee plate, and trying to ignore her former prisoner's hungry gaze.

Earlier, he'd lit the hearth and filled the kettle as though building fires and pumping water were second nature. Somehow, she doubted he'd ever worked as a scullery lad. He probably did everything well. He had that air about him—the air of competence. Self-assurance. Wealth. His clothing was even finer than the thieving solicitor's French suits. And he smelled better than any man she'd ever encountered. He smelled clean.

"There," she said, sliding his cup across the table. "Do ye prefer it sweet?"

"No."

"Have a biscuit or two. Ye seem famished."

"How long were you married?"

She paused mid-sip then answered before finishing. "Two years."

The pure blue of a September sky, his eyes roamed her face before dropping to linger on her bodice. He made her feel naked. "Tell me about your husband."

She winced. "I'd rather not."

"Come, now. Satisfy my curiosity. How did you meet?"

Tapping a fingernail against her teacup, she gazed toward the window. The snow was thickening, the flakes now fat and fluffy. "My cousins and I journeyed to Glasgow searchin' for new employment. He was my last interview."

She began picking apart her ginger biscuit, eating it crumb by crumb. In between bites, she told the story.

"His name was Ross Carmichael. He was a banker seekin' a new housekeeper. I applied for the position at his house on Queen Street. We spent hours discussin' all manner of things—how he preferred tea to strong drink, why he thought walkin' superior to ridin' and thought horses deserved better than to be beasts of burden. He explained his beliefs about payin' female servants the same wage as males. He seemed a wee bit fanciful to me, caught up in his own head. But I'd never had a conversation like that before. He treated me … I dinnae ken. Like he wanted my good opinion, I suppose. He was the worst mistake I've ever made."

"Does that include abducting a duke?"

"Aye."

He drank his tea and arched a brow. "What was he hiding? Let me guess. His high-minded philosophies about women and horses were more rubbish than reality."

She blinked. How did he know? "He was afraid of horses. Refused to keep them."

"And the strong drink?"

"He drank whisky freely enough when somebody else was buyin'. Oh, and not only did he pay the housekeeper less than the male servants, he paid her less than a middlin' chambermaid."

"So, he was a miser."

"Aye. And an embezzler. A cheat. A cruel man whose only interest in compassion was as a means of gainin' an advantage over others."

He took another drink and swept her a leisurely glance. "Why did you marry him?"

"I was a fool. His fool." She glanced down at the crumbs piled on her plate. "Ye might say I've a habit of muddlin' things. I run headlong into decisions before I've had time to think them through. Some of it is misfortune, some just pure miscalculation." She gestured to her bodice with a chuckle. "Or mismeasurement. I've been a burden to my parents since I was wee. Mam was forty when I came along. A big surprise, ye might say. She insists they saw me as a miracle, but it wasnae easy for her or Da. So, when a banker with a house on Queen Street asked for my hand, I couldnae refuse. Bein' his wife meant I could provide for my kin. I could be a boon rather than a burden for once."

Mr. Northfield's hand flexed on the table beside his teacup. He'd done the same in the coach. *Tighten and relax. Tighten and relax. Tighten and relax.* Something about it fascinated her.

"When did he die, Lucie?"

"Come spring, it will be two years." She huffed a hollow chuckle. "Trampled by a neighbor's horse, no less."

"His death was painful, then."

"Oh, aye. Excruciatin'."

"Splendid." He swallowed the last of his tea. She refilled his cup and added two more biscuits to his plate. He nodded his thanks. "Did you inherit anything?" he asked. "The house? Funds?"

She shook her head. "That was my second biggest mistake. Trustin' his solicitor, Mr. Geddes, formerly of Glasgow. Given the fortune he stole, I suspect that whoreson is livin' quite comfortably in France by now."

"You're destitute, then."

She shot him a glare. "That's one way of puttin' it."

"And your family is on the verge of being evicted."

She tossed a gingery crumb into her mouth.

"Frankly, you are your own worst enemy."

"Have I mentioned how bad ye are at offerin' comfort, Mr. Northfield?"

His gaze narrowed. "You need a keeper."

She huffed and began tidying up.

"More to the point, you need a husband."

"No."

"It's the obvious solution."

"No! Never again."

"If you had help in the choosing—"

She braced her hands on the table and leaned forward until her face hovered inches from his. "I will never again put myself at a man's mercy. I've made many mistakes. Too many. But that's one I willnae be repeatin'."

His gaze took on an odd cast, intent and utterly focused. It might be mistaken for coldness, but to her, it seemed more like heat.

Like fire so hot it burned blue.

A wild flurry of shivers cascaded over her skin. Unnerved, she straightened and resumed putting away the tea.

"I can help you," he said, deep and smooth.

"Why would ye do that after I've waylaid ye with a bungled abduction? Most men wouldnae find that endearin'."

"I think your husband filled your head with false beliefs about men. I humbly volunteer my services to correct any such misapprehensions."

She scoffed. "What sort of services?"

"Carnal ones."

Suspended inside a pulsing, pounding, electrifying moment, she felt the world shrink to a single point of focus—Silas Northfield. He sat with catlike stillness, his head slightly tilted, his mouth relaxed into the faintest smile. He was almost lazy in his posture. But that thumb was stroking the rim of his plate. Stroking and stroking and stroking. Soft and repeating. Like the tip of a cat's tail.

She couldn't catch her breath. "I—I dinnae think … I'm not … I thought ye might say ye'd lend me funds or give me a reference. Not … carnal … Dear God."

"Take a breath, love. Slow. Deep. Good."

She followed his direction. It helped.

"Funds would only delay the inevitable," he continued with perfect nonchalance. "A reference might secure employment, but you need more than one woman's income."

He was right. Funds ran out if one had no source to replenish them. And positions for women paid poorly. She needed a permanent home not merely for herself, but for her family. A husband was the time-honored remedy for women in her position. Perhaps her desire to remain unmarried was selfish.

But could she accept such extraordinary assistance from this man? He appeared sincere. His regard was steady enough to brace a bridge. After a few more deep breaths, she said, "Yer offer is very generous, Mr. Northfield."

"Silas will do."

"It's not that I'm ungrateful. But I fear ye'd be wastin' yer efforts."

His mouth took on an amused quirk. "I'm curious why you think so."

Another breath. And another. "I dinnae enjoy … that."

Not a single hint of surprise. "Perhaps I could change your mind about … that."

"Ye have that much time to squander, do ye?" She crossed her arms beneath her bosom. "Honestly, men are bafflin'."

He rubbed the rim of his plate, seeming distracted by her arms. Or something just above her arms.

She glanced down. "Och, more crumbs." As she brushed away the gingery bits, she thought she heard him catch his breath, but when she looked up, he appeared perfectly at ease. "I'm a disaster, Mr. Northfield. Ye've been very kind, considerin' all I've done to ye." He didn't reply, so she clarified, "Forcin' ye to come with me, pointin' a gun at ye, callin' yer mother a whore—"

"Lucie."

"—implyin' ye've an unnatural affection for livestock—"

"I am *not* a kind man."

She begged to differ. He'd been wondrously kind to her, even while hauling her upstairs to the white bedchamber with her squawking and clawing like a maddened hen. Most men would have felt justified in handling her roughly. He hadn't so much as bruised her wrists during the binding. Then he'd held her while she wept. She'd never been held like that, close and tight, yet so careful. Silas Northfield might not see himself as kind, but she did.

"My offer will benefit us both."

She scoffed. "How? It couldnae be pleasurable for ye." She waved at her tall, plumply curved body and overlarge breasts, which pillowed above her neckline. "Just look at me!"

For a long moment, he did. His nostrils flared. His lean jaw flexed. He scarcely blinked. Abruptly, he shoved his plate away and braced his elbows on the table. Briefly resting his forehead on his fists, he drew a breath. When he glanced up, those eyes were flickering oddly. "You'll simply have to trust me on this point."

That was the problem. She couldn't trust him. She couldn't trust any man, apart from her kin. "Where were ye headed when I abducted ye?"

"Carlisle. Then London, I suppose."

She nodded. A wealthy Englishman with such lordly speech and costly boots belonged in London.

"There are two horses in the stable. Take one. Ride back to The Muckle Buck and forget ye ever met me."

"I'm afraid I can't do that."

"Why not?"

"It's snowing heavily. I might lose my way."

She glanced at the window. The world had turned purely white while they'd been having tea, but there was ample daylight, and the road to the inn was well marked.

"We'd best spend the night here," he continued smoothly. "The snow should let up by morning."

"Are ye a cautious man by nature, Mr. Northfield?"

A subtle smile. "More of a planner. Managing circumstances affords me an advantageous position. I do like having the advantage."

"Aye. I've noticed."

"Then we're agreed?"

She sighed. "Fine. Stay here, if ye like."

His grin was slow, sensual, and devastating. In an instant, he went from earthly handsomeness to blinding divinity.

Suddenly, her head felt light and her breath short. How could a man be that beautiful? By all ordinary laws of nature, it should be impossible.

"Lovely," he breathed. "Now, then. Since we'll be alone together, why not give my little proposal a try?"

"I dinnae ken …"

"You've already engaged in much riskier adventures to help your family."

She hesitated. "That's true."

"This is simply a harmless exercise. If it doesn't work, we shall part ways in the morning, no worse for having made the effort."

"I suppose …"

"Lucie. What do you have to lose?"

Her heart squeezed hard enough to wring a bedsheet dry. Nothing. That was the answer. The abduction had been her final act of desperation. In a few days, her family would be removed from the home where she'd been born. After selling their possessions, they'd last a month or two. Three if she found employment immediately. After that … She didn't know.

She swallowed. Her stomach tightened. His "services" probably wouldn't work. He'd be disappointed. She'd be humiliated. They'd both be frustrated. But he was right. She had nothing to lose but a wee scrap of pride—and a moldy loaf of bread was worth more than that.

"Very well, Mr. Northfield. Ye may proceed. Just dinnae feel too badly when it fails."

"Be at ease, love." His grin lit up the kitchen. His eyes shone like the sky. "I expect I'll muddle through."

CHAPTER FOUR

"Ye want me to keep my gown on." Lucie frowned as though he'd told her to wear chicken feathers.

"For now." He continued arranging items around the white bedchamber: lanterns and candles, a looking glass strategically placed for proper viewing, a basin of warm water, and towels. And, of course, the drapery ties.

"Why are ye lightin' so many candles?"

"To see you clearly."

A small silence. "Will ye be undressed, Mr. Northfield?"

He halted beside the bed where she sat gripping one of the spiral posts like a sailor gripping the mast in rough waters. "Would you like me to be?"

Her tongue flickered over that vulnerable lower lip. "Perhaps."

He shrugged out of his waistcoat and untied his cravat. Tossing both aside, he said, "We'll begin with kissing."

"Oh. I havenae done much of that."

For perhaps the hundredth time, he felt like she'd kicked him in the chest. "Tell me what you have done, love."

"I'd rather not discuss that, if ye dinnae mind."

"It needn't be too detailed. I simply want to avoid alarming you with anything unfamiliar."

Her fingers began tapping against the wooden post. She glanced toward the windows then down at her knees. "He called me his dairy maid. Wasnae too keen on this." She gestured to indicate the area from her bosom to her hips. "Told me if I reduced, he'd want me more. But how do ye reduce yer natural form?" Her hands hovered near her bosom before dropping back into her lap. "It wasnae too often that he wanted … that. But when he did, he wanted it fast. He preferred me lyin' on my back. Didnae much care how I felt about any of it. Sometimes, in the middle, he would"—she swallowed as though she might be sick—"flag. That'd make him properly angry."

Anger. Yes, Silas was familiar with that feeling. Felt it right now, in fact. "He blamed you?"

"Aye. Said if I'd do somethin' other than lie there like a plank of wood, such things wouldnae happen."

"Remind me again. His death. Excruciating, you said?"

"Oh, aye. Broken ribs. Punctured innards. Took him days to die."

Silas found the gruesome picture a small consolation. But unreasonable fury still burned like Hades' fire. To distract himself, he stripped off his stock and shirt.

Her gaze riveted upon him, first his chest then his cock. In fairness, the latter was putting on quite a show. Where the bunched fabric of his shirt had previously disguised the pressure on his trousers, now the outline of his shaft was blatantly obvious.

Slowly, her eyes rounded. A tiny crinkle of confusion appeared between her eyebrows. "Is that …" She swallowed. "Are ye certain ye're quite …? Ye seem very … eager."

He huffed out a chuckle. "Yes."

"And big."

He didn't go about comparing his size to other men, but he'd had no complaints. "Does that worry you?"

She shook her head. "Not worry so much as … Might ye have some sort of ailment? One that causes swellin' in unusual places?"

God, she was killing him. "Only if the ailment you're referring to is lust." What in blazes had been wrong with her husband? Everything pointed to him being a rank bastard, but she acted as if a full erection was an anomaly.

"Oh. Well, I'm pleased ye dinnae find me too unsightly." She shifted her hips on the mattress and gripped the post harder. "Good thing ye told me to keep my gown on."

He barely stopped himself from offering reassurances. Words wouldn't help, and she'd only resist him harder. Instead, he held out his hand. "Come join me at the dressing table."

She hesitated before sliding her soft hand into his. He drew her to her feet and led her across the room to the small mahogany table with the large looking glass. He'd placed the basin of water there. Now, he dipped a washcloth into the warm water and asked, "May I?"

She looked puzzled before nodding. "I'm in yer hands, Mr. Northfield. Do as ye please."

For the briefest moment, he thought he might spontaneously come. It was a close thing, and only a lifetime of exacting self-control stopped him. "Oh, love. You shouldn't have told me that."

She shrugged. "Cannae be any worse than …" She swallowed. "Never mind."

Another kick to the chest. At this rate, he'd be lucky to survive the night. "Hold still," he murmured. Then he slid his hand along her cheek, gently bracing her jaw and neck. With the cloth, he cleaned away the dried streaks left by her tears. He pressed the warm, damp linen against her eyes and nose, soothing away the last few signs of her weeping.

Sighing sweetly, she kept her eyes closed and relaxed against his bracing hand. "Ah, that's lovely, Mr. Northfield."

"Silas." He dipped the cloth again before washing her forehead, her cheeks, her gently squared jaw, and finally, her lips. Those parted for him without hesitation. He gave her the tip of his thumb. Her little tongue swiped against it.

A tiny gasp. Another taste.

Hard lust gripped him so painfully, he almost groaned. "There," he whispered instead. "Better?"

With her eyes still closed, she sighed, "Aye."

He tossed the cloth aside and clasped the other side of her neck. Tilting her head up, he lowered his lips to hers. Her tongue flickered out to taste him as she'd done with his thumb. When he responded in kind, she jolted. Her eyes popped open, glinting with sensual wonder. Breathing fast against him, she held his gaze then slowly slid her tongue against his.

His hunger roared a demand. He took her mouth fully, grinding his lips against hers and plunging his tongue deep.

Her sensual moan hummed against his lips. Small, warm hands gripped the sides of his waist just above his trousers.

Pulsing and stroking with his tongue, he buried a hand in her thick, silky curls and gripped to hold her in place. He needed to get deeper. He needed to have more. Her hands grew desperate, her fingers digging into the muscles of his back. He tried to ignore the provocation of her breasts, so soft and luscious, the hard tips pressing her bodice until he could feel them against his naked chest.

Not yet, his instincts warned. *Not yet*. Instead, he devoured her mouth—lips, tongue, delicious flavors of tea and sweet ginger. She was an intoxicating feast, but her mouth wasn't enough. He drew away, fighting for breath, holding her steady.

Slowly, she opened her eyes, those kiss-swollen lips parted and panting. "Silas? I think I like kissin'." The wonder in her voice left him reeling.

He spun her around so her back was to his front then positioned them facing the looking glass. Gathering her spiraling curls to one side, he held her with a fist in her hair and an arm across her waist. Keeping his motions slow and deliberate to set a proper tone without startling her, he nuzzled a spot just beneath her ear. God, she even smelled delicious, like fresh, ripe oranges and warm, spicy cloves.

"This mightn't seem familiar to you, Lucie, but I want you to follow my instructions," he murmured. "Can you do that?"

Her body eased a little more against his. "Oh, aye. Though, I should warn ye, my knees are wobbly. And I'm havin' some sort of reaction. Feels strange."

"Where is the reaction centered?"

Freckled cheeks flushed a deeper pink. Her eyes met his in the mirror. "B-between my legs, mostly."

"How does it feel?"

She swallowed and gripped his arm. "Achy. Empty. Wet."

"You've never felt it before?"

"Alone, sometimes. But never this strong. I think it was the kissin' that did it."

He hid his smile against her neck. "We'll do more. Would you like that?"

She nodded.

"For now, I'd like to see your breasts."

Tension took hold of her. She went still as a stone.

"Remember, you're simply following my instructions," he whispered, holding her hair loosely in his fist and tightening his arm around her ever so slightly. "There's nothing to fear."

He watched her throat ripple on a swallow. He watched her control the anxiousness shining in her eyes. Her fingers dug deeper into his arm, her nails forming painless little gouges. A few heaving breaths later, she rasped, "Very well."

As a reward, he kissed her neck, tracing his tongue along her flickering pulse.

"Are ye goin' to release me so I can remove my gown?"

"No," he said against her soft, lovely, freckled shoulder. He met her gaze in the mirror. "Your bodice is much too tight. Do you see how the velvet strains? It's too much to contain, love. I want you to lower the edge down past your nipples, then let me look my fill."

"I dinnae think ye'll be pleased—"

He wedged a thigh between hers, pulling her into his body harder, higher, tighter. "Let me decide what pleases me."

Oh, she liked that. Satisfaction gripped him as he saw the flush of arousal bloom along her chest and throat and up into her face. Everything about her response told him she *needed* him to take control. The pink heat, panting breaths, and little writhing motions he could feel through her skirts and his trouser leg proved his initial impressions of her nature correct. Her acquiescence only served as further confirmation.

"V-very well." With trembling hands, she pinched the beaded edge of her bodice and dragged it down. And down. And down. It snagged just as the dusky pink of her areolas appeared. She halted, those breasts heaving.

"Keep going," he ordered.

She tugged. Two large nipples—hard, red, and swollen ripe—escaped their constraints to rest upon the black beads.

The hottest hellfire came for him. It roared with beastly force through his body, shaking him to his core. "The rest," he gritted. "Show me."

She was shaking, her exquisite flesh alive with her nervousness and the pounding of her heart. White, freckled, topped by nipples the same ravishing color as her gown, those bountiful breasts were a feast laid before him. She maneuvered them free of their confines, letting them rest atop that obscenely tight red velvet.

"What a vision you are, Lucie." He followed his heated whisper with a tiny nibble of her ear.

She shivered, and her nipples tightened even further. "Ye're still ... still hard." She sounded surprised.

He wedged himself harder against her backside, offering proof of his admiration. "Fancy that. So I am." Another nibble. Another grinding thrust.

She moaned, her head falling back against his shoulder.

"Now, I'm going to let go of you."

"No," she protested, digging into his arm. "Don't."

"Shh. When I do, I want you to go sit on the bed. Do not cover your breasts. Just sit and wait for me. Can you do that?"

A little whimper escaped her throat. "Aye."

He released her hair then, slowly, her waist. Finally, when he was certain she could stand, he backed away. She turned and did precisely as he'd instructed.

By God, this woman was made for him. He needed a moment to regain control; otherwise, he'd devour her like a beast. After a quick splash of water to cool his face, he dispensed with the remainder of his clothing and walked toward her, giving her time to accustom herself to the sight of him.

Those dove-gray eyes fixed upon him, unblinking and utterly riveted to his cock. She repeatedly gripped the bedpost and the edge of the mattress. Her breasts remained flushed and swollen, propped high and round upon their tight velvet nest.

He halted a few feet from her. "There are several ways we can proceed, Lucie. I shall give you three options. You must choose one."

"What if I dinnae care for any of them?"

"Choose one, and we'll take it slowly. I haven't frightened you yet, have I?"

"No. I was surprised when ye … but no. Ye havenae frightened me."

He nodded. "Good. All the options involve you permitting me certain liberties with your body without interference. Your breasts are my preference, of course. That's option one."

She frowned. "What's option two?"

"I'd like to explore that lovely little garden between your legs."

"Explore?"

"Mmm. Thoroughly."

Blinking, she huffed out a disbelieving chuckle. "Why would ye want to fuss about down there?"

"You'll understand better after I'm finished with you."

Her expression was skeptical. "And option three?"

"You seem curious about this." He waved to the massive erection making every drawn breath a pulsating torture. "If you'd like a closer inspection, I will allow it, though the same rules apply. You must let me guide you without interference."

"Can I use my hands?"

"No."

She gave a disgruntled grimace. "Doesnae seem fair."

"It isn't. But this is how it must be."

"Fine. I'll take option three."

He retrieved one of the drapery ties.

"What's that for?"

He looped the soft cording around one of her wrists. "If you lose control, this will bind both hands."

She snorted. "Lose control. Aye, right."

"Keep your hands at your sides. I'm going to let you have a look. But you mustn't touch until I say so."

She gripped the edge of the mattress and nodded. "I'm ready."

He moved close, holding his shaft before her eyes and tightening his muscles against the urge to simply fall upon her and … but he couldn't. She needed everything he could give her. The patience. The control. The restraint. So, he stood and let her look her fill.

And she looked bloody enchanted. "It's splendid, Silas. Those veins look very swollen. Does it hurt?"

Another kick to the heart. "It aches, much the same way you described earlier."

She licked her lips and weaved forward, drawing closer to the rounded tip. Her breath scalded him. "Oh! It moved."

"Yes," he said tightly. "It does that."

"May I … May I kiss it?"

Bloody hell. "Very well. Take it slowly—dear *God,* woman." He braced a hand against the bedpost as her lips skimmed the tip's edge. Her tongue darted out, curious and flickering to taste the small bead of fluid welling for her. And, just as he'd anticipated, her eager little hand came up to grip his shaft and hold him in place as she began to suckle and taste. She rubbed the shaft against her cheek as though savoring him.

"Feels like hot silk. Ye're so hard, Silas. Hard and beautiful."

He gripped the bedpost hard enough to crack the wood. Abruptly, he knew he wouldn't last much longer. He clasped her wrists and bound them loosely at her back, just enough to remind her to keep her hands under control. Then, amid her pouting protests, he cupped her face, kissed her deeply, and said, "Now, we move on to option one."

"But I—"

He started to lay her down.

"Option two!" she shouted. "I'd rather option two."

The lustful drumbeat of his heart nearly drowned her out. He clenched his fists on the mattress. He gritted his teeth and hung his head for long breaths. "Right. Option two."

Sliding to his knees, he inched her skirts up, tracing the long, curvaceous lines of her legs. Higher and higher, he went. The silken skin beyond the stocking, the hot, damp wonders of her steamy folds. She hadn't been exaggerating how wet she was. He shoved her skirts up to her waist then spread her thighs wide.

He couldn't stifle his deep, agonized groan. What an exquisite creature she was. Flushed crimson and glistening with need, those soft petals were pleading for his mouth. He gave them his fingertip.

She gasped.

He gave her a light stroke. And another. A dozen more. He found the sweet bud inside her dark nest of curls. Skimmed it with his thumb. Her opening seized and fluttered.

She fell back onto her elbows, her back arching and her breasts beautifully prominent in his vision. "Silas?" she panted. "I think I'm havin' another reaction."

"Would you like to have my fingers inside you?"

She grunted, her head falling back as her nipples tightened even further. Her answer was a long, tortured moan. "Aye."

His longest finger slid inside her tight sheath. She soaked his hand as ripples seized and seized and seized. Tighter and tighter. He gave her another finger. Then he lifted her legs onto his shoulders and dipped down to suckle her swollen clitoris. Her screams of ecstasy echoed off the white walls, soothing something ravenous inside him. For the first time in his life, he felt like he was being fed.

She was his nourishment. Her surrender. Her pleasure.

Obsession took hold. He wanted more. He suckled harder, using his tongue to flicker, play, and torment her. He curled his fingers and found a particularly sensitive place inside her sheath. Then he added pressure.

Another round of throaty screams. Another flood of sweet nectar. Another deeply satisfying climax.

He grew greedy. He wanted more. More and more and more. He drew back to admire his work. That sweet little nub was swollen, scarlet-red, and exquisitely prominent above where his fingers penetrated her.

He felt her hand in his hair and glanced up. She'd freed herself and now lay gazing at him with both wonder and trepidation. "Silas, I cannae. Not again."

He kissed her inner thigh, savoring the sweet essence of her on his tongue. "We haven't addressed option one yet, love."

Her head shook as she sobbed his name.

"Shh," he soothed. "Your body needs this." He supposed that was true, but he also needed it. Like a starving man, he needed to feast.

Slowly, he lapped at her clit, drawing out her continuous peaks until she was begging him for mercy. She gripped his hair and tugged. He ignored the sharp sensations for a while, but soon, her desperate pleas penetrated the thick fog in his head.

"Please, please, please," she chanted. "Silas, I cannae bear it." Her lovely gray eyes were damp.

He shook his head and frowned. Stilled. "Bloody hell," he rasped. "Did I frighten you?"

"No," she choked. "But it's too much. I want to kiss ye again."

His gaze dropped to her breasts. Gently, he slid his fingers free, savoring her sweet gasp as he gave her swollen bud a soft nudge. "I've much more to do, love." He painted her nipples with her spicy-sweet nectar.

She gripped his hair harder with one hand while she tried to shove herself up with the other.

He controlled her movements by gripping her waist. "Be easy," he murmured. "I haven't steered you wrong yet, have I?"

She stilled, her breaths heaving like a dainty bellows. "No?"

He grinned at the question in her tone. "Then let me steer."

It took a long while for her to nod, but when she did, everything inside him roared with satisfaction. With swift, smooth motions, he lifted her legs onto the bed, turning her to lie with her head on the pillows. He lay beside her and arranged her hands to rest beside her shoulders. "Keep them there, love."

She nodded, her gaze soft and vulnerable.

He stroked her cheek and kissed her mouth, savoring her sweetly feminine groans. "Look at me," he commanded.

She opened her eyes and held his.

He directed her gaze down to his cock. "You see how much I want you?"

Swallowing hard, she replied, "Aye. I can see that."

"Good. Keep watching." He splayed her legs wide, settling her skirts above her waist so that her lovely scarlet folds were open and visible. Then he stretched out alongside her, stroking her cheek and giving her small, nibbling kisses. "Take another look. Am I still hard?"

She blinked. "Aye. I want to kiss it again."

His cock leapt. Wept. Nearly erupted. "No."

She moaned and writhed. "But I want it so badly, Silas."

He closed his eyes and summoned whatever scraps of control he had remaining. Those scraps were tattered and thin. "I know."

"Cannae ye allow me a wee taste?"

"I'm going to touch your breasts, now."

Her expression turned mulish. She turned her face away.

With gentle fingers, he nudged her gaze back to him. "Watch me." With that, he dipped his head down to the tantalizing, freckled mounds so beautifully prepared for his pleasure. He nuzzled her with his chin. Lapped her with his tongue. Drew her tightly beaded nipple into his mouth and suckled as hard as he dared.

She arched high, forcing her breast deeper into his mouth. He cupped her, controlled her, nibbled and suckled and watched her quake. Then he switched to her other breast, sucking the ripe tip deep before giving her the edge of his teeth. She seemed to need a nearly painful pressure, so he gave her that, too, testing her limits and watching her little clit flush and swell.

She gripped the pillows and moaned his name, but she didn't pull away. She didn't close her legs. She didn't try to stop him. And, he noticed, she kept looking at his cock, which raged to be inside her. It gave him an idea.

He withdrew, murmuring to soothe her agitation. Then he sat up and rolled to his knees beside her. Cupping her cheek with one hand, he brushed her lips with his thumb. Next, he took his cock in hand and forced the head down to brush her nipple.

Her moan was long, high, and sweet. He sank his thumb inside her mouth while brushing the tip of his cock against her nipple over and over. She went wild, groaning and writhing, her eyes darkened into a storm cloud by intense arousal.

He pushed her harder, his starvation feeding deeply on the first real nourishment he'd ever had. Her pleasure was both wine and sustenance, intoxication and satisfaction. Suddenly, he felt the edge of his control hurtling closer. He stilled. Gritted his teeth. Closed his eyes. "Bloody hell," he hissed.

"Silas?" she gasped. "What's wrong?"

"I have to fuck you now."

"Oh." Pause. "Aye. Th-that's fine."

He pulled away, hanging his head and breathing. "You don't understand. My control is … slipping. It may be fast—"

In an instant, she'd rolled onto her knees and cupped his face between her hands. She forced his gaze to hers.

He could scarcely breathe.

"It's fine," she whispered, kissing his mouth. "I want ye inside me."

A deep, anguished groan escaped him. Why had he delayed so long? The answer came swiftly—because her desire was a feast, and he was a greedy, starving man.

She drew him into her arms and pulled him down to lie on top of her, stroking his hair and wrapping her legs around him. Then she put her lips to his ear and said the one thing capable of breaking him: "Come inside, Silas. I need ye."

CHAPTER FIVE

The man in Lucie's arms was impossible. He simply could not be.

Nobody should want her this much. Nobody should be this patient, this arousing, this skilled. He knew too much about her body—things she'd never suspected. He knew how she'd feel before she felt it. At every turn, he'd waited for her to trust him before proceeding. At every turn, he'd exercised perfect control over her, but more importantly, over himself.

A man like this shouldn't exist. And now, she knew he didn't. At least, not without limits. Because his perfect control had finally broken.

She didn't mind in the slightest. In fact, she quite preferred him this way—red-faced, wild-eyed, shivering with urgent, desperate need.

Aye, she liked this Silas Northfield very much, indeed.

He fell upon her like a ravenous beast, kissing her with deep, desperate thrusts of his tongue. No more methodical calculation. Just gripping hands, harsh breaths, and hard, heavy weight. He gathered her hair in his fist and buried his lips against her throat. "Lucie," he gritted. "Forgive me."

He entered her with a long, savagely deep thrust. It felt nothing like she'd expected. But then, he was significantly larger than her husband.

The magnitude of him filling her all at once stole her breath. There was no pain. Just monumental pressure, heat, and stretching fullness. Immediately, he began thrusting. Long, hard, emphatic thrusts. His chest abraded her nipples with every motion. Those sensitive tips were tender from his mouth, as was the little nub of flesh between her thighs. He'd suckled it so hard that it remained distended above her folds. She'd been shocked to see herself earlier—her breasts, her womanly mound. She'd felt like a pagan offering, her body foreign and fully ripe. Now, as he rocked inside her sheath, his thick stalk brushed against the spot he'd made swollen and tender.

Lightning sizzled through her. She dug her fingers into his back, arched against him, and seized hard. He did it again. She screamed. Clawed. He clasped her wrists and pinned them above her head with one hand while cupping her breast with his other. His hips drove harder and harder.

She struggled against the spiraling pleasure. It gathered like a storm with flashes of lightning streaking through her nipples and the place where they were joined. "Silas," she sobbed.

He raised his head, those blue eyes maddened as they held hers. "Give in," he growled. "Give me what I'm craving, love."

The world turned white as pleasure exploded in a pulsating blaze. Distantly, she heard him groan and felt the heat of his mouth around her nipple. Her body wrung his with cataclysmic force. Releasing her breast, he clasped her knee and pressed her legs wider to hammer inside relentlessly hard. Over and over, faster and faster, until finally, he held her fully at his mercy while he pounded to a stunning culmination.

The explosion detonated. Her breath stopped. Both of them released agonized shouts of sensual bliss at the same moment. She realized her hands had been freed some time earlier, and automatically, she reached for him.

He collapsed upon her with his full weight, his muscles shuddering and flexing in ebbing waves, his face buried in her neck. His hands repeatedly clawed into the bedding. She couldn't see his face, only feel his harsh, desperate breathing.

She held him gently, sensing that this had been shattering for him, too. "Shh," she soothed, stroking his hair and his back, savoring the fullness of him still inside her. "Rest, now. Ye've done as ye promised." She turned her head to kiss his jaw. "Though, I think ye may have ruined me for other men."

Slowly, he relaxed, his body easing toward sleep. His heated weight, his closeness, and the rhythm of his breathing all led her toward sleep, as well. As she drifted off to the sounds of the crackling fire and the blustering snow, she thought he whispered something against her skin. Something odd and familiar.

"Ah, love. You shouldn't have told me that."

She awakened with him still inside her. He was hard as steel and lodged deep. He strummed her nipple with his thumb and stroked her hair. As she opened her eyes, she saw him gazing at her with blue-fired intensity.

"There you are," he murmured. "I've been waiting."

She panted. Shifted. Moaned. "Aye?" Laying her hands on his chest, she marveled at the texture of springy blond hair and hot, hard muscle. "I can feel ye have." She grunted as he began to move. Slow. Steady. In and out. Deep and deeper.

"Too much?" His question was as nonchalant as a man asking if he'd poured too much whisky into her glass.

"No." She breathed and tilted her hips. Doubtless she'd be sore in the morning. "Ye're ... not exactly a small man, are ye?"

He grinned, those blue eyes dazzling in the firelight. "What can I say? You whet my appetite."

She chuckled and caressed his shoulders, his neck, his jaw. "That's not all I'm wettin'."

His fingers tightened on her nipple, and his rhythm picked up speed. His expression shifted from playful to focused. "Come for me, Lucie."

Astonishingly, within three strokes, she did. Her peak expanded like a bubble, swift and hot. She clung to him, wrapping her arms around his neck and crying his name against his skin.

He scooped both arms beneath her, crushing her against him and holding himself deep and still to let her finish. After long, lingering kisses and a great deal of petting—she noticed how much he liked to play with her hair—he resumed his prior steady pace.

She groaned.

"Too much?"

"Good God, Silas," she panted. "I thought ye'd be ready to finish."

This time, his grin was tinged with wickedness. "Don't be silly, love. We're just getting started."

She wore his shirt—and nothing else. She read him her speech to Dingwall with passionate sincerity. She complained about her hair being unruly. She laughed as she teased him about looking hungry all the time. She took his hand as if they'd never spent a day apart. She led him down to the kitchen and fed him ginger biscuits with her fingers. She didn't complain when he seduced her into lying on the table or when he feasted on her like a man obsessed.

In fairness, he was precisely that: a man obsessed with a freckled Scottish woman who smelled like ginger and cloves.

He'd kept at her all night, and she'd yet to deny him. Indeed, she was intoxicatingly eager. He'd been trying to restrain himself, but it was difficult. He'd gone hungry for a long time.

Now, sitting near the fire in the white bedchamber, Silas pulled her onto his lap and wrapped a dark, rich curl around his finger. Her hair fascinated him. He liked to bury himself in it and breathe her in.

She caressed his neck, traced his lips, and sighed. "I ken nothin' about ye. Do ye realize that?"

He nuzzled her ear, savoring the warmth of her backside against his thighs. "What do you wish to know?"

"Tell me about yer kin."

He arched a brow. "Are you asking about Dingwall? He's not my family. We're half-brothers, but neither of us acknowledges the blood tie."

"No, I wasnae askin' about him. Though, I'm not sure how ye aim to keep such a secret, considerin' the resemblance."

He chuckled. "People see what they choose to see. We have another half-brother, incidentally. Francis Prescott, Lord Medford. He's the legitimate one."

She traced a finger over his brow. "Ye sound as if ye like him better."

Another grin took him by surprise. He'd smiled more since he'd met her than he'd done in the past five years. "Francis is difficult not to like. Believe me, I tried."

He explained their meeting six months earlier. He'd been bitter after his mother had tearfully informed him that his father was not his sire, that she'd made dreadful mistakes early in her marriage, and that his father was the kindest, most honorable man on the face of the earth.

"Medford was a reprehensible bastard," he clarified. "Peter Northfield is the man who raised me. He accepts me as his heir, and he's been quite clear on this point: I am his son in every way that matters." He shrugged. "Mama is right. He's an extraordinary man. I could not be that forgiving."

"He must love you and yer mam very much."

He hummed his agreement. "He's known from the beginning, though they hid the truth from me and refused to give the rumors any air to breathe. When Francis paid Mama a visit, the whole sordid tale emerged. Gin was involved, apparently. Copious weeping. Descriptions of a prurient nature. I was profoundly grateful to have been absent. Francis wasn't so lucky. In any case, Mama later insisted that he and I endeavor to form a brotherly bond. His mother and my mother were once friends, you see."

"Oh. Until yer mam …"

"Yes. Dallying with another woman's husband tends to strain the friendship. Mama has a sentimental nature. She longs for a reconciliation."

"But she got her wish with ye and Francis," she said. "Ye speak of him like a brother."

"His charm wears away all resistance, much like water upon a stone. He refuses to concede until even the coldest heart has warmed to him. I think he saw me as a challenge."

Lucie frowned. "Ye dinnae have a cold heart."

He kissed her lips, her nose, her temple. Sweet Lucie. He'd correct her, but he didn't want to frighten her away.

Fortunately, she changed the subject. "What were ye doin' with Dingwall at The Muckle Buck?"

"Francis inherited several properties he finds distasteful. They're the houses where the late Lord Medford kept his mistresses. Rather than sell, he's decided to transfer ownership to Medford's ill-begotten progeny. When Francis contacted him, the Duke of Dingwall expressed an interest. Francis was headed to the Highlands to spend Christmastide with friends.

Dingwall was headed to England for similar purposes. We set a meeting."

"Were ye accompanying Dingwall?"

"God, no. I can scarcely tolerate the man."

"So ye traveled with Francis. From London?"

He nodded.

"But ye werenae headed to the Highlands when I waylaid ye. Ye were headed back to London."

Another nod.

"Ye traveled from London to Scotland for a meetin' with a half-brother ye cannae tolerate, just to turn round and go back to London." She shook her head. "I dinnae understand."

"What's to understand?" He smoothed a spiral of her hair between his fingers. God, she smelled good. Spiced and womanly.

"Christmas is days away."

"And?"

"Did ye have nothin' better to do than traipse across England to enjoy our fine Scottish weather?"

He played with one of the ties of his shirt, which draped fetchingly over her right breast. "No, I suppose not."

"Where did ye plan to spend Christmas, Silas?"

"Somewhere on the road between here and London, likely."

"Alone?"

He shrugged. "I'm often alone."

"At *Christmas?*"

What a peculiar question. "All year round, really."

She fell quiet. Then her hand clutched his and held it against her heart. "Silas Northfield," she whispered.

Startled, he met her gaze. Her eyes were welling. Her lower lip was trembling. What the devil? "What are you doing? Lucie. Don't weep. Stop right this instant."

A tear welled up and overflowed. Another. And another.

He panicked. He must stop her. What had he done last time? Bloody hell. He scooped her up and carried her to the bed. After dropping her on the mattress, he lay down with her, gathered her close, and squeezed her hard against his body. "I don't know why you're crying, but you must cease immediately."

She sniffled and wiped her nose on his sleeve. "I cannae help it." Her palm flattened over his heart.

"Yes, you can. Try holding your breath."

"Ye're very bad at comfortin'."

"My talents lie elsewhere. Ask me to hunt you a lion in Africa. Or draft a bill for the Prime Minister. Or teach you how to load a bloody pistol."

She released a damp chuckle. "Or turn me into a wanton lass. Ye do that without even tryin'."

He threaded a hand through her hair and drew her even closer. She thought all this was unintentional? God, she needed a keeper.

She laid her cheek on her hand, which rested over his heart. "Ye must come home with me before ye return to London. Mam and I will make dumplings and tatties. Da will share his whisky. I'll not have ye starvin' so near to Christmas."

He didn't know why she'd made the offer, and he didn't care. She could not have furthered his plans any better if she'd read his mind. Thankfully, she couldn't perform such a trick, or she would have fled the moment he'd caught sight of her in her red dress.

As calmly as he could manage, he said, "I shall come with you on one condition."

Sniff. "That I stop weepin'?"

"Yes. Also, another helping of option two. I'm feeling peckish."

She laughed. Moaned. And reached up to whisper against his lips, "Only if I can have a wee bit more of option three."

"You drive a hard bargain, Lucie Carmichael. But I think we can settle on those terms."

CHAPTER SIX

"**A**re you ready?" Silas asked from the passage to the entrance hall.

Sighing, she stared out at the bright white snowfall. "It's a bonnie place, this. Such big windows, and so many. The house on Queen Street was dark and narrow. A townhouse, ye ken? The neighbors were always arguin'. Here, it's quiet. Peaceful."

He came closer, setting her valise down beside their feet and wrapping his arms around her from behind. She noticed how much he enjoyed holding her, as though it fed him, somehow.

"We'll ride to the inn," he murmured in her ear. "Then we'll hire a carriage. It's seven miles, yes? Shouldn't take us more than an hour."

She nodded, swallowing a lump. She didn't know what her parents would think about her failure to prevent the eviction or about the man she'd be bringing home. But it didn't matter. She longed to see them. And if they understood what Silas meant to her, then they'd love him, too. She didn't know how she'd be able to let him go when the time came.

Fortunately, she didn't have to face that heartbreak today. There was ample daylight remaining for travel, and a visit with her family could extend into tomorrow. They were starting late. Having slept hours longer than Silas, she'd awakened after half the day was gone. She'd washed quickly and scrambled to dress. After tea, Silas had prepared the horses while she'd tidied up, doused the fires, and eliminated all signs of their presence.

It took less than a quarter-hour to reach The Muckle Buck and another twenty minutes for Silas to secure a coach. He strode into the inn's dining room after she'd finished eating a warm stew. She glanced up and smiled softly. "How handsome ye are, Mr. Northfield," she murmured as he reached her side. "I dinnae ken how I'll manage when ye're …" She swallowed her next words, but the ache in the pit of her stomach was harder to suppress. She must regain control of herself. Silas hated seeing her weep. She didn't want to distress him. "Are ye hungry?"

Unsmiling and intensely focused, he pulled her to her feet. "The coach is waiting. We should go."

She nodded and followed him outside. In the yard, she blinked at the grandeur of the coach he'd hired. "Ye couldnae find a smaller one?"

"I wanted you to be comfortable." He bundled her into the luxurious carriage before seating himself across from her and signaling the driver. The coach lurched forward. Calmly, he dusted snow from his overcoat and retrieved a blanket for her from a basket near his feet.

She frowned. "Silas? Is there somethin' amiss?"

He raised a brow. "Amiss?"

"Ye seem tense."

"I'm perfectly calm."

"Aye. Calm. But tense. Like ye're waitin' for an adder to bite."

"Perhaps I'm anticipating a lovely afternoon with your family."

She glanced out the window at the thick sheet of white blanketing the landscape. "Well, it should be enjoyable. Da's eyesight isnae too keen, but he kens how to play a fiddle. Douglas will be there, and Rabbie, too. Oh, and I'll show ye the pond where I broke my ankle one summer. A sore injury. I healed, of course, but not before I'd grown fat on Mam's shortbread. She bakes for me whenever I'm feelin' nervy. That's another thing ye'll enjoy. Mam's dumplings are …" She frowned as they passed a familiar signpost. She craned her neck to look behind them. "Silas?"

"Yes, love."

"I think yer driver is goin' the wrong direction. We're headed toward Gretna."

Silence.

She focused on his face. His beautiful, utterly calm face. "What—what are ye doin'?"

"We are going to Gretna."

"Why?"

"To meet your family."

"My family lives north of here. North of The Muckle Buck. Most certainly north of Gretna."

More silence. More calm. A hint of triumph. He looked like a cat after a successful day's hunting.

"No," she breathed.

"Yes."

"Ye cannae."

"I am."

"This is …?"

"An abduction." His grin was slow and deeply satisfied. "Settle in, Lucie Carmichael. You've been taken. And soon, you'll be mine."

On the day she was abducted, Lucie wept a total of seven times. The first time was when she spotted her mam and da waiting outside the white blacksmith's shop in Gretna. She stumbled out of the coach before it stopped moving and ran to embrace them. Da, being nearly blind, shouted her name as soon as he heard her speaking. Mam blotted her tears and held her tightly and fussed over her "fine lad" with the fair hair and blue eyes.

The second occurrence happened when Da explained how they'd traveled there so quickly. "Ye see, it was the Duke of Dingwall. He paid us a visit this mornin'. And it's the strangest thing, Lucie-lass. He's sold the house, but the new landlord doesnae want us to leave. Isnae that somethin'?" Da looked a wee bit sheepish. "I confess I didnae think yer plan would work, but I was wrong. Ye brought him round in the end and found ye a fine new lad in the bargain."

Mam interjected, "Aye, His Grace looked disheveled." She motioned drinking from a bottle and rolled her eyes. "He had signs of havin' been mauled by a woman, but we didnae ask about it, just in case ye were to blame."

The third bout of weeping happened when she interrogated Silas about Dingwall's change of heart. "How?" she uttered, clinging to his coat after Mam and Da had gone inside to speak to the blacksmith. "How did ye do this? And when? And … how?"

"I knew he'd be at the inn, so I rode there while you were sleeping and rousted him for a conversation. We had words. I offered a small compensatory property in exchange for your family home. He agreed. I stipulated certain conditions—the use of his coach, the passing along of a message. And there you have it."

She narrowed her eyes upon him. "How wee was this compensatory property?"

He shrugged. "Sufficiently that I shan't miss it. Francis may balk. I promised him its use for summer sea bathing. But there are more than enough castles dotting the English coastline for such purposes. He can purchase one of his own."

She collapsed into his arms, wept uncontrollably, and earned herself stern commands to cease at once, followed by a crushing, panicked embrace. "For God's sake, woman. I don't have a bed for us to lie upon. You must stop."

Her fourth and fifth bouts of weeping came when Silas Northfield presented his case for why she must marry him.

"You need a keeper. And I'm keeping you."

"Oh, Silas."

"Do not start again. You just finished—no. Lucie, I'm quite serious. Do not—ah, bloody hell. Come here."

A short while later, she regained control, only to have it collapse upon hearing Silas's argument for why he was a cold-hearted bastard whom, under normal circumstances, she'd be mad to marry because he would be "the sort of husband who's forever after you to satiate his hunger." He paused. "However, you must consider the very real possibility that you're carrying my child."

She grew weak, her knees wobbly. Hovering a hand over her belly, she stared at this miraculous man with alarm and wonder. "Do ye think it's possible?"

"I should hope so. I went to a great deal of trouble in the effort."

She argued that he'd be entangling himself with a habitual bungler and that he didn't have to marry her to have done the right thing. He'd already done far more for her and her kin than she would have dared ask.

He told her to hush. Then he kissed her. When they both came up for air, he reminded her that she'd been thoroughly compromised, and the required remedy was marriage. She protested that she didn't want him to feel trapped. He asked whether she understood the meaning of "abduction" or "mine." She laughed. He didn't.

The sixth bout of weeping happened during their wedding ceremony after the blacksmith struck the anvil and declared them married. She stood with her new husband, nose red, eyes puffy, red dress too tight, her throat tied in a knot of shifting emotions. Silas looked at her as if she were a ravishing beauty. He kissed her in front of everyone. When he was done, tears flowed down her cheeks. "How handsome ye are, Mr. Northfield," she whispered tightly, cradling his jaw. "Is it any wonder why I fell in love?"

His eyes flared the brightest blue. He stared at her for a long while before saying, "I will always wonder, Mrs. Northfield. But so long as you have reasons in mind, I shall endeavor to be deserving of such a gift."

The seventh bout of weeping came hours later, after he carried her across the threshold of Hartfell Lodge. "The solicitor said we may take possession immediately," he explained, gently setting her down in the white bedchamber and quickly lighting a fire. "The sale should be completed within a month."

Earlier, while they were celebrating their nuptials with her family at The Muckle Buck, Silas had spoken with a wiry, hairless gentleman covered in snow. He'd explained that Dingwall employed the same solicitor who was managing the estate sale of Hartfell Lodge.

He'd sent a note to the man's office in Carlisle early that morning.

"Do ye trust this solicitor?" She squinted her skepticism.

"I regard him as anyone should regard a solicitor—with great caution and loathing."

She smiled slowly and set about unfastening his coat. "Are ye a very cautious man, Mr. Northfield?"

"More calculated, really. Caution implies I hesitate when I see something I want."

She smoothed her hands over his chest and raised up on her toes to kiss him. "And ye wanted this place."

"I want you. Hartfell Lodge is merely a way to entice you to remain by my side."

She eyed her new wedding ring, a gold band with diamonds and sapphires. "I should think havin' married me would accomplish that aim."

He began plucking the pins from her hair, looking fascinated and focused. "Francis once told me how to recognize when you've found the right companion to walk through life with. He said to look for someone who gladdens your heart simply by entering a room, then make that room the one where she most wants to remain."

Her eyes welled. She fought against it, but her heart had been in a constant battle all day. "Aye?"

His eyes met hers, glowing like a boundless September sky. "Every room is better for having you in it, Lucie Northfield. And if you'll choose to stay in mine, I promise to spend every day making certain you're glad for having chosen well."

She cradled his face between her hands and drew him down for another kiss, though it was made damper by her tears. She laughed as he gently caressed them away. "I think ye're improvin' at this comfortin' business, my love."

He grinned, taking her breath away. "Am I?"

"Aye. And as for where I'd prefer to stay, that's simple." She laid her palm over his heart. "I'll stay right here forever. There's no place I'd rather be."

Watch for the next book in the
Midnight in Scotland series

COMING SOON!

MIDNIGHT IN SCOTLAND: BOOK FOUR

THE WICKEDNESS
OF A HIGHLANDER

BY

ELISA BRADEN

MORE FROM ELISA BRADEN

*Be first to hear about new releases, price specials,
and more — sign up for Elisa's free email newsletter at
www.elisabraden.com so you don't miss a thing!*

Midnight in Scotland Series
*In the enchanting Midnight in Scotland series,
the unlikeliest matches generate the greatest heat.
All it takes is a spark of Highland magic.*

THE MAKING OF A HIGHLANDER (BOOK ONE)
Handsome adventurer John Huxley is locked in a land
dispute in the Scottish Highlands with one way out: Win the
Highland Games. When the local hoyden Mad Annie Tulloch
offers to train him in exchange for "Lady Lessons," he agrees.
But teaching the fiery, foul-mouthed, breeches-wearing lass
how to land a lord seems impossible—especially when he
starts dreaming of winning her for himself.

THE TAMING OF A HIGHLANDER (BOOK TWO)
Wrongfully imprisoned and tortured, Broderick MacPherson
lives for one purpose—punishing the man responsible. When
a wayward lass witnesses his revenge, he risks returning to
the prison that nearly killed him. Kate Huxley has no wish to
testify against a man who's already suffered too much. But
the only remedy is to become his wife. And she can't possibly
marry such a surly, damaged man…can she?

THE TEMPTATION OF A HIGHLANDER (BOOK THREE)
Hunted by a madman bent on possessing her, English beauty
Clarissa Meadows flees to a friend's house in the Scottish
Highlands. With nowhere left to run, she accepts the
protection of rough, solitary giant Campbell MacPherson. But

falling for her bodyguard puts him in a predator's sights, forcing an impossible choice: stay with the man she loves or save him from the wolf she's brought to his door.

RIGHT PLACE, WRONG DUKE (NOVELLA)
Widow Lucie Carmichael has made too many mistakes in her life, but she's not about to let the Duke of Dingwall evict her family from their ancestral home, even if that means engaging in a little abduction. Silas Northfield is *not* the Duke of Dingwall, no matter how much a mad Scottish lass insists he is. So, when she abducts him, Silas takes matters—and the luscious Lucie—into his own hands.

Rescued from Ruin Series
Discover the scandalous predicaments, emotional redemptions, and gripping love stories (with a dash of Lady Wallingham) in the scorching series that started it all!

EVER YOURS, ANNABELLE (PREQUEL)
As a girl, Annabelle Huxley chased Robert Conrad with reckless abandon, and he always rescued her when she pushed too far—until the accident that cost him everything. Seven years later, Robert discovers the girl with the habit of chasing trouble is now a siren he can't resist. But when a scandalous secret threatens her life, how far will he go to rescue her one last time?

THE MADNESS OF VISCOUNT ATHERBOURNE (BOOK ONE)
Victoria Lacey's life is perfect—perfectly boring. Agree to marry a lord who has yet to inspire a single, solitary tingle? It's all in a day's work for the oh-so-proper sister of the Duke of Blackmore. Surely no one suspects her secret longing for head-spinning passion. Except a dark stranger, on a terrace, at a ball where she should not be kissing a man she has just met. Especially one bent on revenge.

THE TRUTH ABOUT CADS AND DUKES (BOOK TWO)
Painfully shy Jane Huxley is in a most precarious position, thanks to dissolute charmer Colin Lacey's deceitful wager. Now, his brother, the icy Duke of Blackmore, must make it right, even if it means marrying her himself. Will their union end in frostbite? Perhaps. But after lingering glances and devastating kisses, Jane begins to suspect the truth: Her duke may not be as cold as he appears.

DESPERATELY SEEKING A SCOUNDREL (BOOK THREE)
Where Lord Colin Lacey goes, trouble follows. Tortured and hunted by a brutal criminal, he is rescued from death's door by the stubborn, fetching Sarah Battersby. In return, she asks one small favor: Pretend to be her fiancé. Temporarily, of course. With danger nipping his heels, he knows it is wrong to want her, wrong to agree to her terms. But when has Colin Lacey ever done the sensible thing?

THE DEVIL IS A MARQUESS (BOOK FOUR)
A walking scandal surviving on wits, whisky, and wicked skills in the bedchamber, Benedict Chatham must marry a fortune or risk ruin. Tall, redheaded disaster Charlotte Lancaster possesses such a fortune. The price? One year of fidelity and sobriety. Forced to end his libertine ways, Chatham proves he is more than the scandalous charmer she married, but will it be enough to keep his unwanted wife?

WHEN A GIRL LOVES AN EARL (BOOK FIVE)
Miss Viola Darling always gets what she wants, and what she wants most is to marry Lord Tannenbrook. James knows how determined the tiny beauty can be—she mangled his cravat at a perfectly respectable dinner before he escaped. But he has no desire to marry, less desire to be pursued, and will certainly not kiss her kissable lips until they are both breathless, no matter how tempted he may be.

Twelve Nights as His Mistress (Novella – Book Six)

Charles Bainbridge, Lord Wallingham, spent two years wooing Julia Willoughby, yet she insists they are a dreadful match destined for misery. Now, rather than lose her, he makes a final offer: Spend twelve nights in his bed, and if she can deny they are perfect for each other, he will let her go. But not before tempting tidy, sensible Julia to trade predictability for the sweet chaos of true love.

Confessions of a Dangerous Lord (Book Seven)

Known for flashy waistcoats and rapier wit, Henry Thorpe, the Earl of Dunston, is deadlier than he appears. For years, his sole focus has been hunting a ruthless killer through London's dark underworld. Then Maureen Huxley came along. To keep her safe, he must keep her at arm's length. But as she contemplates marrying another man, Henry's caught in the crossfire between his mission and his heart.

Anything but a Gentleman (Book Eight)

Augusta Widmore must force her sister's ne'er-do-well betrothed to the altar, or her sister will bear the consequences. She needs leverage only one man can provide—Sebastian Reaver. When she invades his office demanding a fortune in markers, he exacts a price a spinster will never pay—become the notorious club owner's mistress. And when she calls his bluff, a fiery battle for surrender begins.

A Marriage Made in Scandal (Book Nine)

As the most feared lord in London, the Earl of Holstoke is having a devil of a time landing a wife. When a series of vicious murders brings suspicion to his door, only one woman is bold enough to defend him—Eugenia Huxley. Her offer to be his alibi risks scandal, and marriage is the remedy. But as a poisonous enemy coils closer, Holstoke finds his love for her might be the greatest danger of all.

A Kiss from a Rogue (Book Ten)

A cruel past left Hannah Gray with one simple longing—a normal life with a safe, normal husband. Finding one would be easy if she weren't distracted by wolf-in-rogue's-clothing Jonas Hawthorn. He's tried to forget the haughty Miss Gray. But once he tastes the heat and longing hidden beneath her icy mask, the only mystery this Bow Street man burns to solve is how a rogue might make Hannah his own.

Once Upon a Midnight Kiss (Novella)

Charming antiquities dealer Andrew Farrington relies on his clumsy-but-capable private secretary, Euphemia Sinclair, to be there when he needs her. But when she travels to Scotland in search of a family heirloom only a married woman can claim, Andrew will do anything to keep this indispensable woman by his side—including marrying her before she marries someone else.

The Oddflower Series
Suitors beware: The season of wallflowers is about to begin.

The Secrets of a Moonlit Night (Novella)

Sinister rumors of the mysterious Half-Faced Man haunt the ruins of Northcliffe Abbey. But governess Elizabeth Nightingale knows claptrap when she peddles it. So, when the real Half-Faced Man—architect Thomas Warwick—warns her to keep her young charges away from his property, Elizabeth isn't frightened by his scars. She's frightened by how easily he sees through her disguise to the woman beneath.

ABOUT THE AUTHOR

 Reading romance novels came easily to Elisa Braden. Writing them? That took a little longer. After graduating with degrees in creative writing and history, Elisa spent entirely too many years in "real" jobs writing T-shirt copy ... and other people's resumes ... and articles about giftware displays. But that was before she woke up and started dreaming about the very *unreal* job of being a romance novelist. Better late than never.

Elisa lives in the gorgeous Pacific Northwest, where you're constitutionally required to like the colors green and gray. Good thing she does. Other items on the "like" list include cute dogs, strong coffee, and epic movies. Of course, her favorite thing of all is hearing from readers who love her characters as much as she does. If you're one of those, get in touch on Facebook, Instagram, and Twitter or visit **www.elisabraden.com**.